Read for Me, Mama

To my mother and father, who read to me.
—V. R.

To Camille, my daughter, who loves to read.
—L.M.E.

Text copyright © 1997 by Vashanti Rahaman
Illustrations copyright © 1997 by Lori McElrath-Eslick

Published by Caroline House
Boyds Mills Press, Inc.
A Highlights Company
815 Church Street
Honesdale, Pennsylvania 18431
Printed in China

Publisher Cataloging-in-Publication Data
Rahaman, Vashanti.
    Read for me, mama / by Vashanti Rahaman ; illustrated by Lori McElrath-Eslick.—1st ed.
[32]p. : col. ill. ; cm.
Summary : A young boy who loves to read helps his mother on the road to literacy.
ISBN 1-56397-313-8
1. Reading—Fiction—Juvenile literature. 2. Literacy—Fiction—Juvenile literature.
[1. Reading—Fiction. 2. Literacy—Fiction.] I. McElrath-Eslick, Lori, ill. II. Title.
    [E]—dc20   1996   AC   CIP
Library of Congress Catalog Card Number 95-77784

First edition, 1997
Book designed by Tim Gillner
The text of this book is set in 15-point Palatino.
The illustrations are done in oils.

10 9 8 7

Read for Me, Mama

by Vashanti Rahaman

Illustrated by Lori McElrath-Eslick

Boyds Mills Press

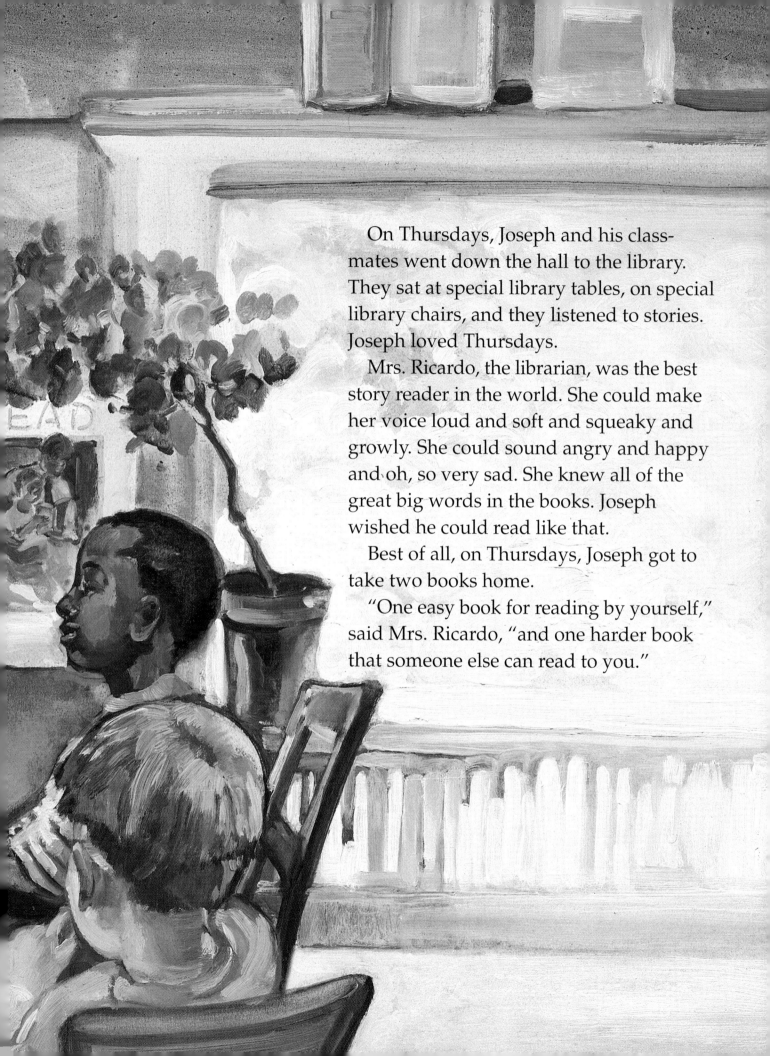

On Thursdays, Joseph and his class-
mates went down the hall to the library.
They sat at special library tables, on special
library chairs, and they listened to stories.
Joseph loved Thursdays.

Mrs. Ricardo, the librarian, was the best
story reader in the world. She could make
her voice loud and soft and squeaky and
growly. She could sound angry and happy
and oh, so very sad. She knew all of the
great big words in the books. Joseph
wished he could read like that.

Best of all, on Thursdays, Joseph got to
take two books home.

"One easy book for reading by yourself,"
said Mrs. Ricardo, "and one harder book
that someone else can read to you."

At home, Joseph put his books on the kitchen table and found the snack Mama always left for him. He read the easy library book and watched his favorite television show. It was about kids' books. They had different books on the show every day, and Joseph tried to remember their names. Maybe some of the books from the show would be in his school library.

When Mama came home, she gave Joseph a
hug and a kiss even before she took off her coat.

"You okay, little man?" she asked. "What
happened with you today? Anything to tell
your mama?"

"Today was library day," said Joseph. "Mrs.
Ricardo read us a funny story. But she can't tell
stories as good as you."

Mama was the best storyteller in the world.
Her voice danced and played with the words.
She could make the most ordinary things seem
not so ordinary after all.

While Mama fixed supper, she told Joseph about her day. She told about the big bird's nest the painters found in the bank sign near her bus stop. She told about the pumpkin vine that was taking over the empty lot, covering up all the ugly garbage. She told about the pot of geraniums someone had put in the deep hole in the sidewalk. She told about the people who were nice to her in the big hotel where she cleaned the rooms. There were nice people there, and people who were not so nice.

When all the dishes were washed and the apartment was clean, Mama and Joseph went out. They went out every day except Fridays. On Mondays, they went to the grocery store. On Tuesdays, they went to clean house for old Mrs. Holder whose hip hurt too much. On Wednesdays, they went to church choir practice. And on Thursdays, they went to the laundromat.

Joseph always took his library books to the laundromat. While the clothes were in the washer, he read the easy book once more. While the clothes were in the dryer, he looked at the pictures in the harder book.

Joseph's favorite harder books were about zoo animals. He wished he could read all the words.

"Do you suppose the book tells what they feed those animals?" asked Joseph.

"You can ask Mr. Beharry," said Mama. "Look, he's coming now."

Mr. Beharry was a university student who lived in a room above the laundromat. He didn't talk much to the other people. But with Joseph and Mama he was not so quiet.

"How's my best buddy?" he would ask Joseph. And they would talk and laugh together.

Mr. Beharry did his laundry on Thursdays, too. He always came just before Mama's clothes were dry. He put his clothes in a washer and then, while Mama folded her laundry, he read the harder book to Joseph.

Mr. Beharry didn't read loud and soft and squeaky and growly like Mrs. Ricardo. He didn't read angry and happy and oh, so very sad. He read slowly and pointed at the words with his finger so Joseph could follow. Sometimes, they even found words and sentences in the hard book that Joseph could read himself.

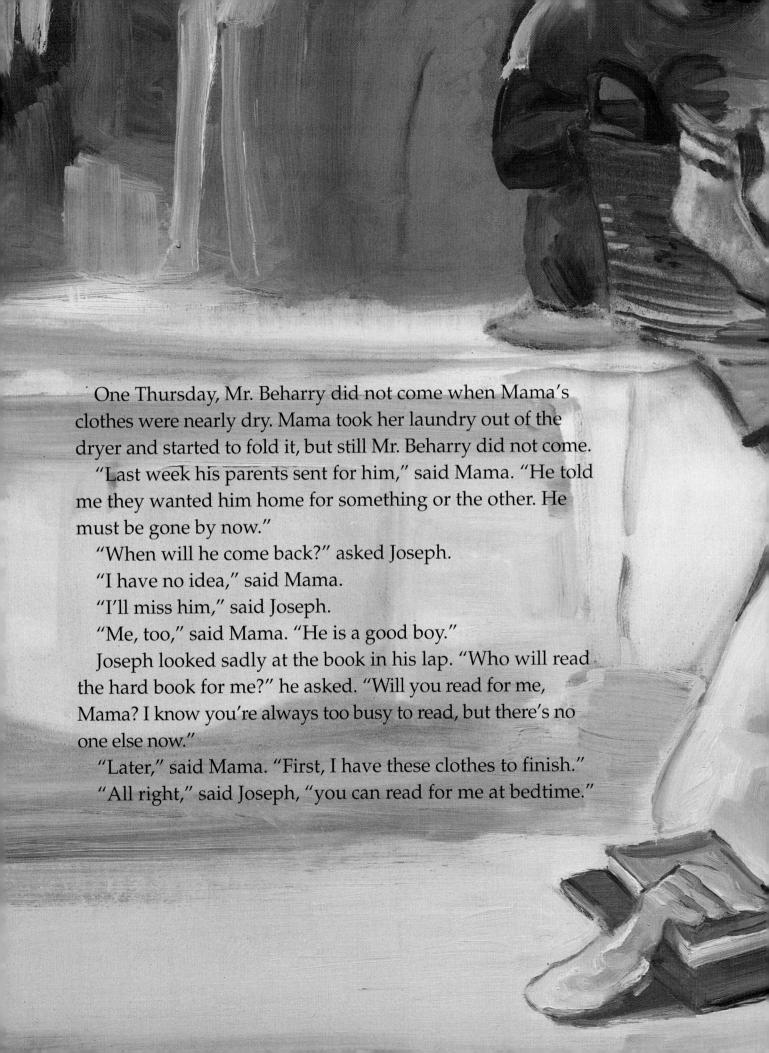

One Thursday, Mr. Beharry did not come when Mama's clothes were nearly dry. Mama took her laundry out of the dryer and started to fold it, but still Mr. Beharry did not come.

"Last week his parents sent for him," said Mama. "He told me they wanted him home for something or the other. He must be gone by now."

"When will he come back?" asked Joseph.

"I have no idea," said Mama.

"I'll miss him," said Joseph.

"Me, too," said Mama. "He is a good boy."

Joseph looked sadly at the book in his lap. "Who will read the hard book for me?" he asked. "Will you read for me, Mama? I know you're always too busy to read, but there's no one else now."

"Later," said Mama. "First, I have these clothes to finish."

"All right," said Joseph, "you can read for me at bedtime."

But at bedtime, Mama said, "It is too late, now. Look at you! You are so tired, you can hardly stay awake!" She kissed Joseph gently and tucked him into bed.

"Read for me, Mama," said Joseph on Friday evening. "It is not too late, and I'm not tired yet."

"Friday evening is when I clean the bathroom and scrub the floor," said Mama. "It is the only time I have to do that."

"I forgot," said Joseph. "But tomorrow you work in the morning only. You can read for me tomorrow when you come home after lunch."

On Saturday afternoon, Mama came home later than usual. Joseph ate the lunch she had left for him and waited and waited. He was worried. Mama had never left him alone for so long before. What if she was hurt or lost? It was almost suppertime when Mama came back.

"Poor child!" she said. "Poor child!" And she hugged Joseph and kissed him and hugged him again. "You all right? You ate your lunch? You didn't get too frightened?"

"It's okay, Mama," said Joseph. "I ate everything. I'm not frightened now that you're home."

"Poor child!" said Mama again as she took off her coat. "I don't know how this happened. They changed the work sheet and changed my work times. I didn't know. I didn't see the sign they put up about it, didn't know there was a sign about it. But don't worry. Next Saturday we'll get old Mrs. Holder to stay with you. I'm sorry, little man. I'm very, very sorry."

Joseph was just happy that Mama was safe. He couldn't understand why Mama kept fussing.

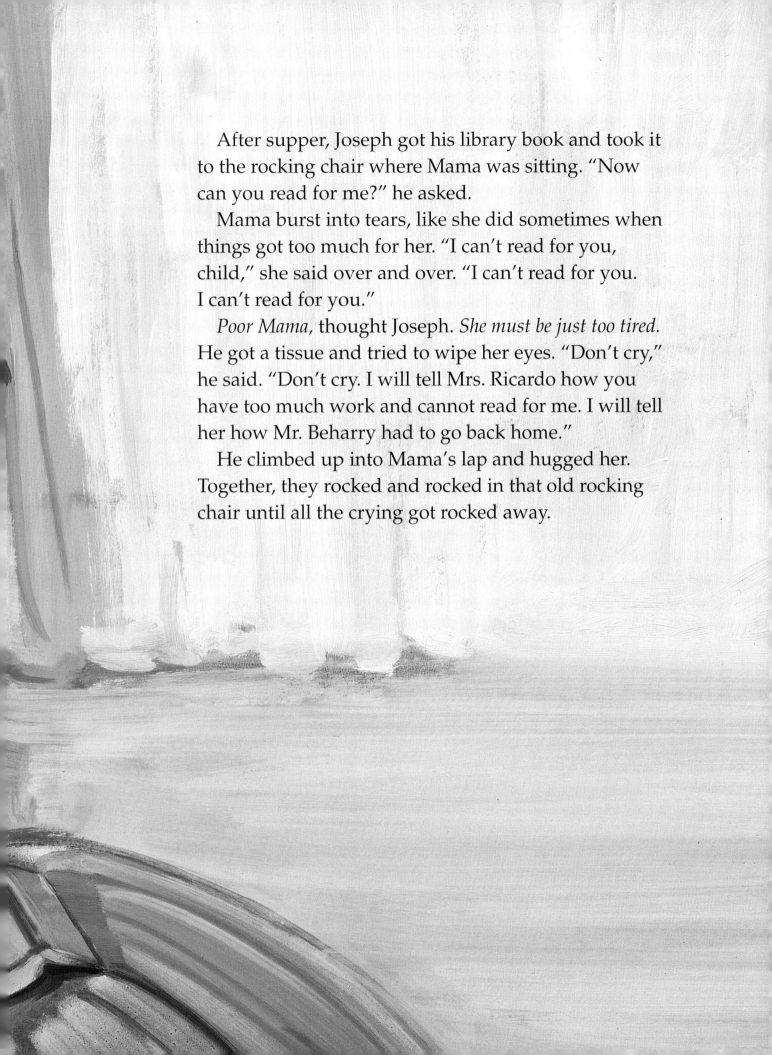

After supper, Joseph got his library book and took it to the rocking chair where Mama was sitting. "Now can you read for me?" he asked.

Mama burst into tears, like she did sometimes when things got too much for her. "I can't read for you, child," she said over and over. "I can't read for you. I can't read for you."

Poor Mama, thought Joseph. *She must be just too tired.* He got a tissue and tried to wipe her eyes. "Don't cry," he said. "Don't cry. I will tell Mrs. Ricardo how you have too much work and cannot read for me. I will tell her how Mr. Beharry had to go back home."

He climbed up into Mama's lap and hugged her. Together, they rocked and rocked in that old rocking chair until all the crying got rocked away.

On Sunday evening, Joseph and Mama went to church. Mama was the best singer. She knew the words of all the hymns. She didn't even have to use the hymn book.

After the singing, the preacher asked if there was anything anybody wanted to pray about.

To Joseph's surprise, Mama got up. "I have to learn to read," she said. "My boy needs a mama who can read. But I never practiced up my reading, never learnt it good in school, and it all got lost from my mind, all got lost."

"Send her help," said the preacher as he began to pray.

But Joseph didn't hear the rest of the prayer. He was too surprised at what Mama had said. Mama was so smart and brave, maybe she just forgot how to read because she had to work so hard. Maybe he could help Mama. But how could he help?

Outside the church, a big girl came up to Mama and told her about the vocational school. They had evening classes there to teach grown-ups how to read.

"I learned to read there myself," said the big girl.

After that, Joseph brought his work home from school every day. When Mama came home, he showed it to her. He read all the words and pointed at them with his finger so Mama could follow.

And on Fridays, after supper, Mama went to reading class.

Joseph went, too.

At first, Joseph sat next to Mama in her class. Then he stayed in the room with the other kids whose mamas and papas were learning to read.

They would play games, and draw, and make things. There was a lady there who read to the children. Joseph would bring his library books along, and she would read them out loud. But she did not read as well as Mrs. Ricardo or Mr. Beharry. So Joseph still took his books to the laundromat on Thursdays. Mr. Beharry might come back one day.

One Thursday evening, while the clothes were drying, Mama picked up Joseph's harder library book. She turned the pages and studied them and smiled. "This is a nice book," she said. "Come, look at it with me. Listen to what it is about."

Almost bursting with excitement, Joseph listened as Mama talked about the pictures in the book. She didn't talk like Mrs. Ricardo. She didn't talk like Mr. Beharry. She didn't even talk like Mama.

Slowly and carefully, Mama's voice stepped from word to word, page after page after page. Mama was reading!